SUPER DUPER

Penny   Pru   Cyril   Loz

WALKER BOOKS
AND SUBSIDIARIES
LONDON · BOSTON · SYDNEY · AUCKLAND

For Laurie

PENGUIN SLIDE

Kipp   Carlos   Pauline

LEONIE LORD

The penguin family are setting off
on an epic journey.
Big ones at the front,
small ones at the back.
Hmm. They seem to know exactly
where they're going...

I like that about Penguins.

WADDLE

WADDLE

The penguins are patiently waiting for a bus ...

and still waiting and waiting for a bus ...

and when the bus finally comes...

They all have their tickets ready.
Penguins are pretty well-organized, you know!

This is their stop –
the station!
When it comes to escalators,
penguins will always stand on the
right so that busy sea turtles
can get past.

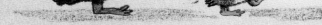

Now the penguins have to be quick - they've got a train
to catch! Of course they have their tickets ready,
and of course they know exactly where they're going.

All aboard ...
and mind the gap.

Chugga chugga, choo choo!

But sometimes things don't go entirely to plan.

The train terminates here due to nesting guinea pigs on the line. Everyone must get off the train!

Oh no, penguins!

What are you going to do *now*?

Baby guinea pigs are sleeping!

shhhh!

But then they remember ...

THAT THEY ARE PENGUINS.

And as well as being patient, organized and polite,
penguins are persistent, too!
Penguins never, EVER give up.

QUIET
PLEASE

You will never hear a penguin complain about the rain,

or the snow,

or ask "are we there yet?"

And when it looks like they just can't go on...

A penguin is never too proud
to phone for help.
And a goat will always know
the best way up a mountain...

YES

YES

YES!

The very top of the one and only…

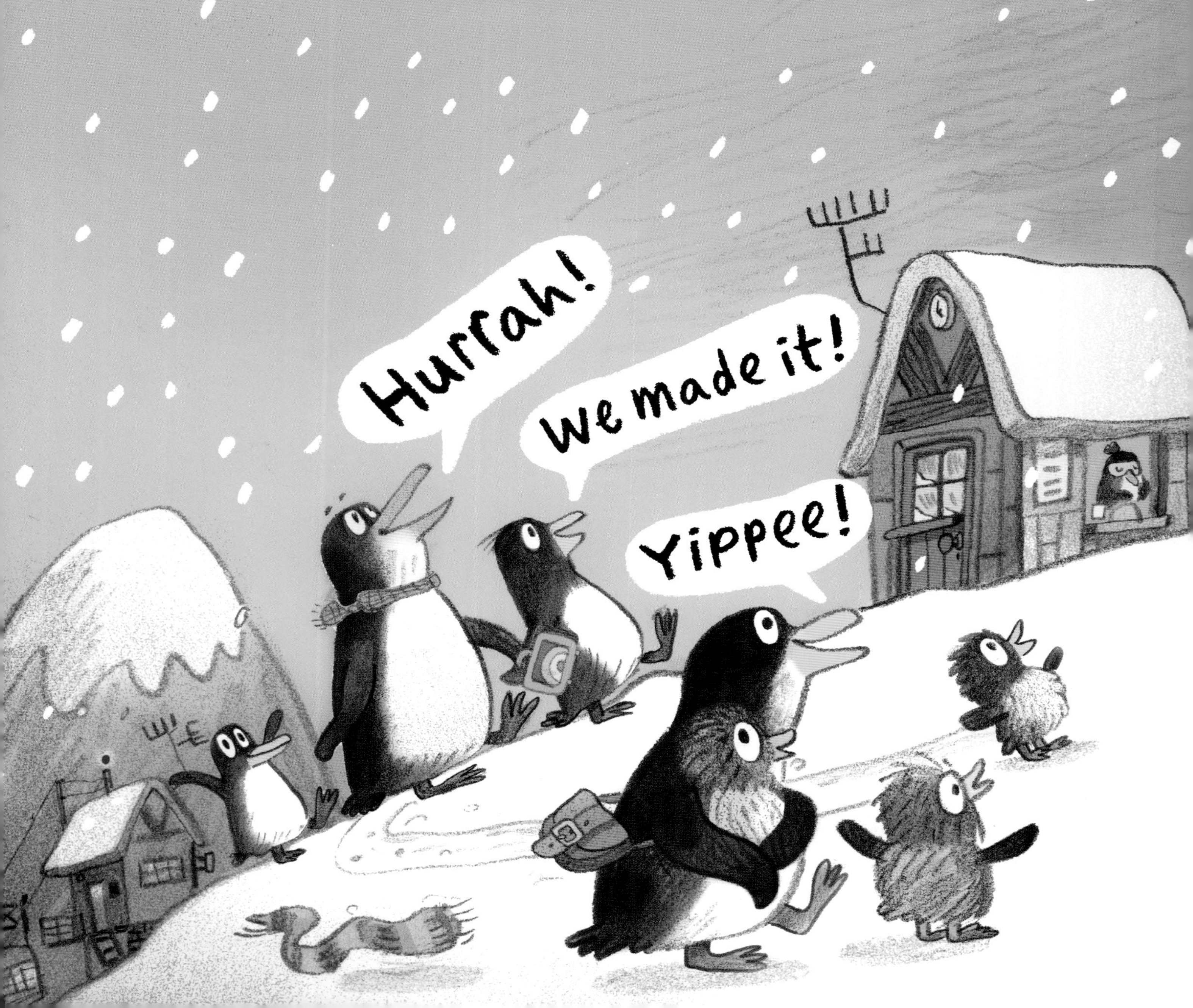

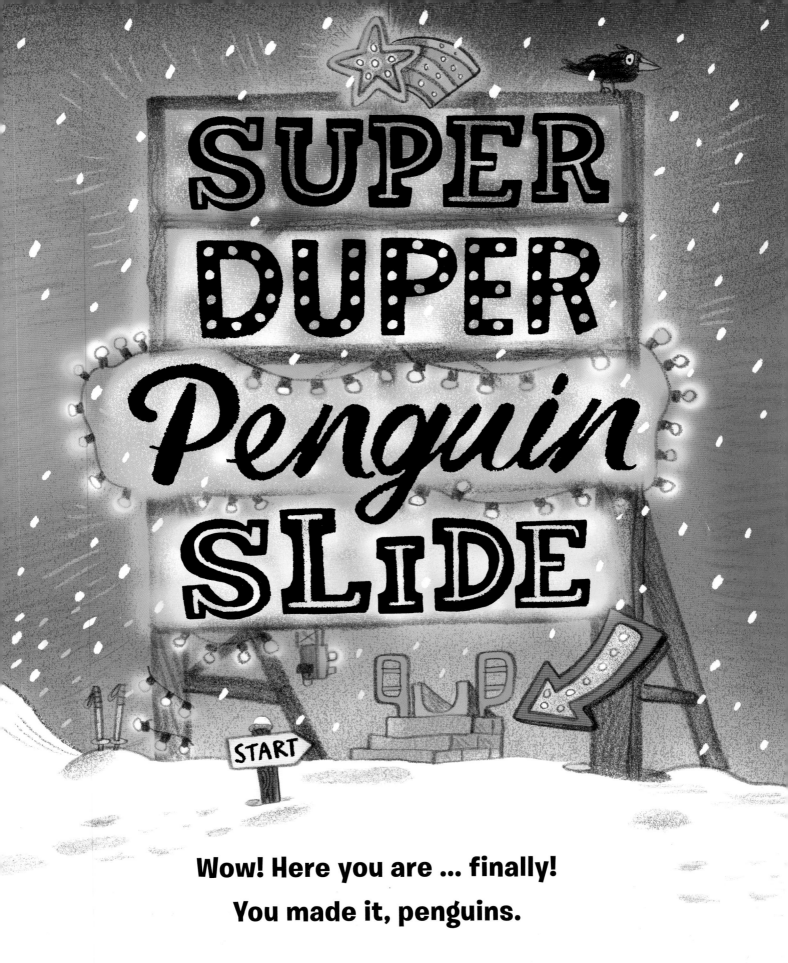

Wow! Here you are ... finally!

You made it, penguins.

OK, keep your flippers in,

line up one at a time,

and wait for
the green light...

Now GO, penguins,
GO,
GO,
GO!

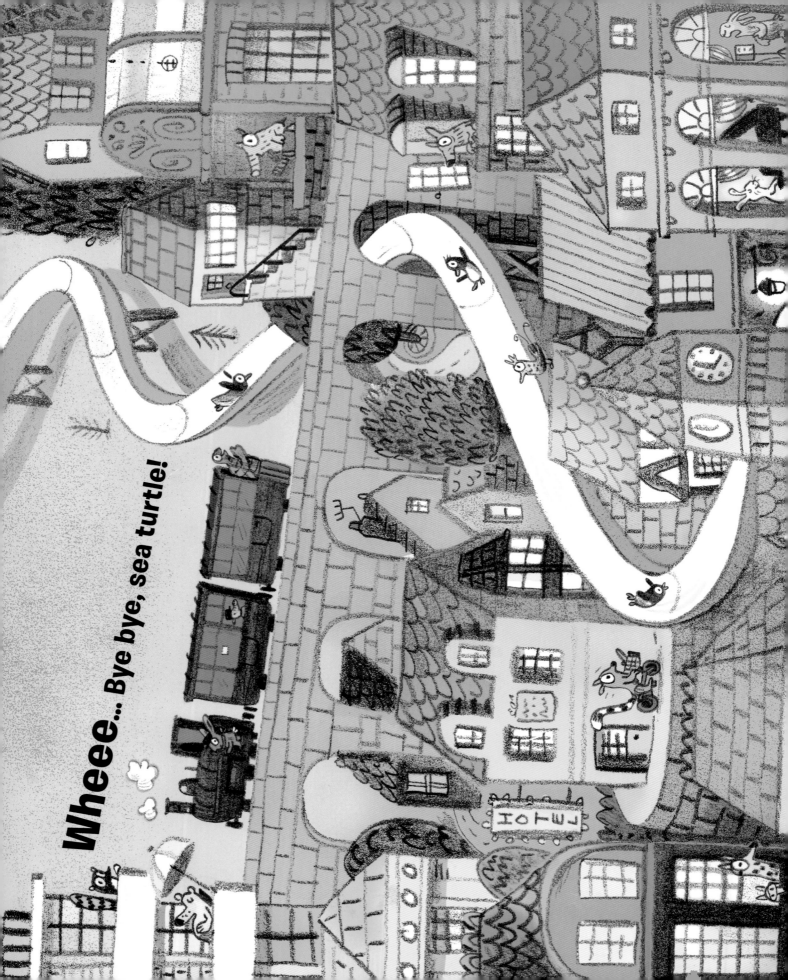

Wheee... Bye bye, sea turtle!

All the way back home.

And when the little penguins squark
"AGAIN AGAIN AGAIN!"
What do you think their big penguins say?

"Come on then!"

Big ones at the front, small ones at the back.
Oh, I do like that about penguins.